This book is dedicated to the selfless donor who made the decision to be an organ donor and gave my father a second chance at life. There is no greater gift. My family will continue to celebrate your legacy each and every day.

-*Author, Casana Fink*

There were three bears, Papa Bear, Mama Bear, and Baby Bailey Bear, who lived in the charming town of Critterville.

This is their story.

One day, Papa Bear was not feeling very well.

Zippy the Zebra came by to see how the sweet Bear family was doing.

"Hi Bailey," Zippy greeted his friend. "I came to check on your dad. I heard he was not feeling well."

"Hi, Zippy. Sadly, he's not," Bailey replied. "He was rushed to the hospital and told that his liver isn't working anymore."

“Oh no! What is a liver, Bailey?”

“A liver is an organ in the body. It works like a filter. It helps clean bad things out of your blood,” Bailey explained.

“Wow!” exclaimed Zippy. “That sounds important. So how can the doctors help Papa feel better?”

“Well, the doctors said he needs a liver transplant or he will pass away,” Bailey said with a frown.

“What is a transplant?” asked Zippy.

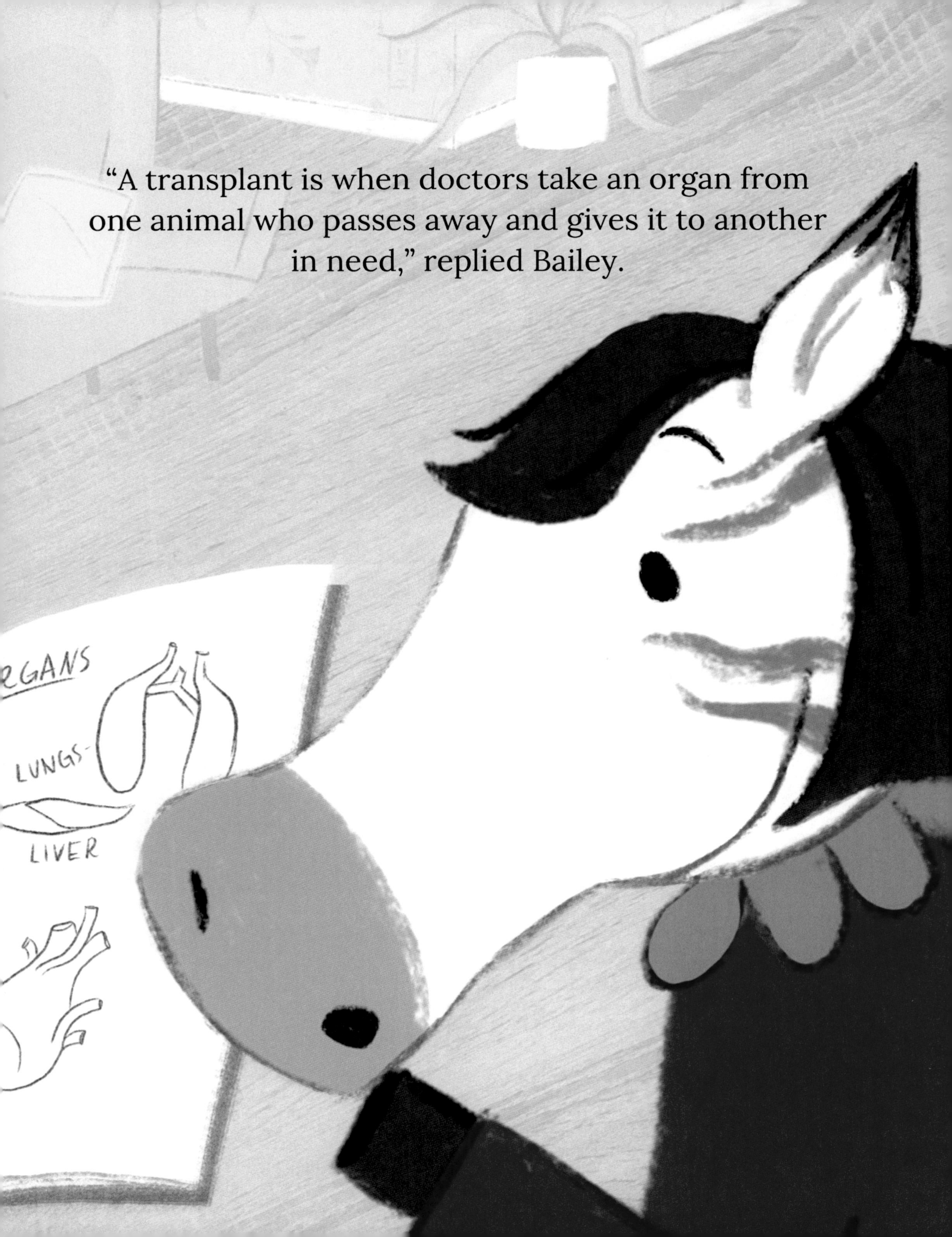

"A transplant is when doctors take an organ from one animal who passes away and gives it to another in need," replied Bailey.

“Do you remember when Gerry the Giraffe passed away?” Bailey asked, “It was very sad.

Before he passed, he told his family he wanted to be an organ donor.

Because of his kindness, the doctors were able to use his organs to save animals in Critterville.

That is how I learned how important organ donation is.”

"That is such a special gift!" exclaimed Zippy.
"Will getting a new liver heal Papa?"

"Yes, once he gets a new liver from a donor, he will slowly get healthier and stronger like before."

"Papa will go on to live for many more years because another critter decided to be an organ donor and give the gift of life," Bailey said with a grin.

“Are there other organs that can be
donated?” asked Zippy.

“Yes! There are six organs that can be
donated,” Bailey replied.

“Oh wow!” Zippy exclaimed.
“What are they?”

“They are the kidneys, liver, lungs, heart, pancreas,
and intestines,” explained Bailey.

“Are there a lot of critters in need of organ transplants like Papa?” asked Zippy.

“Yes!” answered Bailey. “Over 100,000 critters are waiting for life-saving organ transplants right now.”

“Wow! That sounds like a lot!” Zippy replied.

Bailey nodded, “That many critters could fill every seat in the largest football stadium or the Colosseum! That is more than all the critters in Critterville.”

+100,000
LIVES

“So being an organ donor can save many lives?” Zippy asked.
“Yes,” Bailey replied. “One organ donor can save up to
eight different lives.”

"But Bailey, there are only six organs,” Zippy said confused.
“How can eight lives be saved?”

“That is a great question, Zippy! There are two lungs, two
kidneys, one heart, one pancreas, one intestine, and one liver.
You have two lungs, two kidneys, and one of everything else -
that equals eight!” Bailey said excitedly.

"That is amazing!" replied Zippy. "One selfless decision can not only save the life of someone you love but many lives. How can I help save lives?"

"Well Zippy, there are a few things you can do. You can sign up to be an organ donor when you get your Driver's License, or you can tell your family you want to be an organ donor if you pass away. You can also be a living donor," explained Bailey.

"A living donor?" Zippy questioned. "What is that?"

"A living donor is someone who gives an organ while they are still alive. As a living donor, you can donate a kidney or part of your liver," Bailey replied.

“You have taught me so much, Bailey,” Zippy exclaimed.
“I am going to sign up to be an organ donor today!”

Bailey smiled and said, “Great idea, Zippy!
Remember, to be an organ donor is to give the gift of life. I will always be grateful that the kindness of a stranger saved the life of someone I love.”

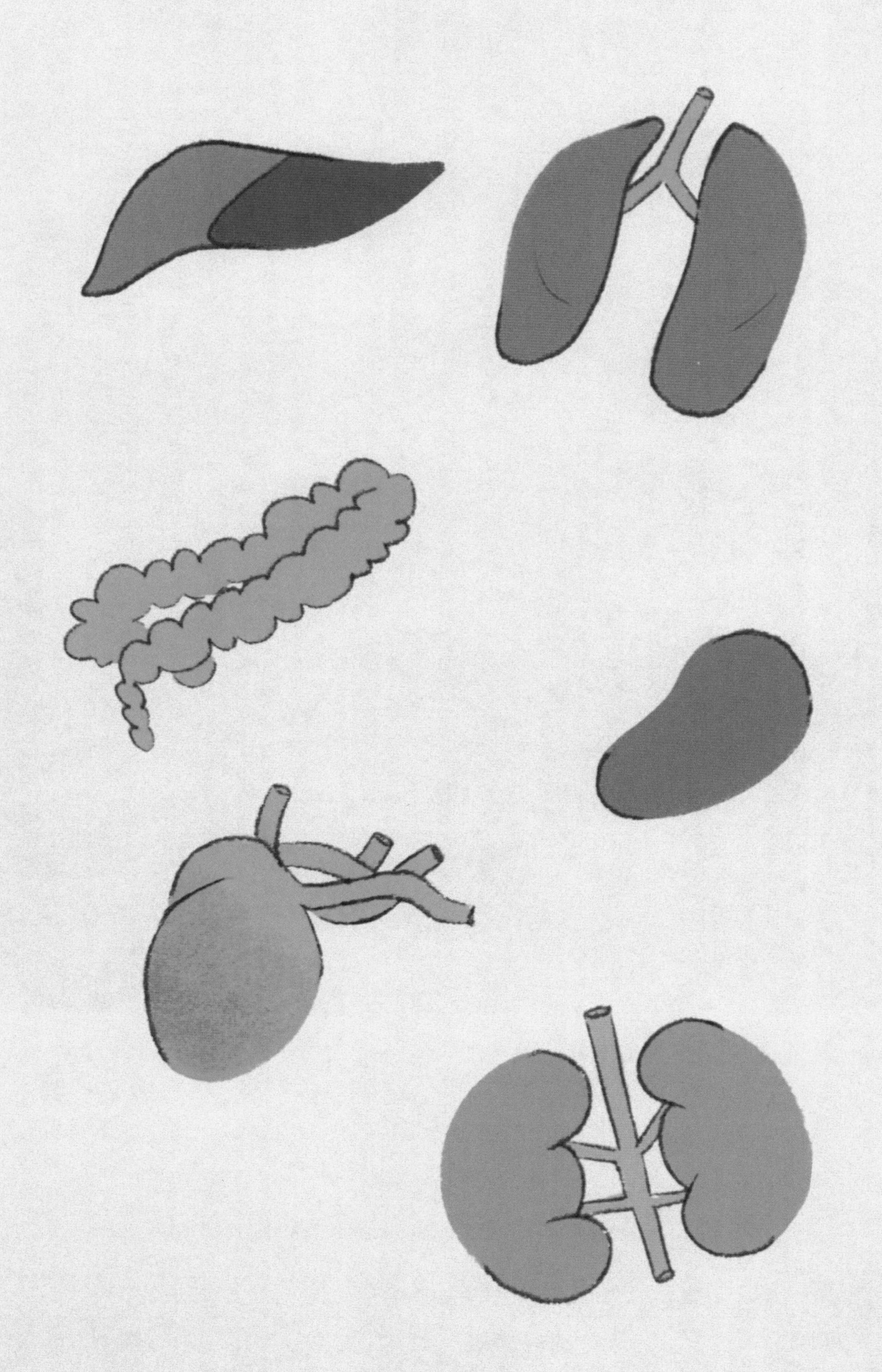

100,000+ people are currently waiting for
an organ transplant in the United States.

Every 10 minutes someone is added to the
organ transplant waitlist.

On average, 17 people pass away each day waiting for a
lifesaving organ transplant.

One organ donor can save up to 8 lives.
All ages can donate.

There is no financial cost to your family to be a donor.
As a living donor, you can donate a kidney or part of
your liver.

You can register to be an organ donor at
DonateLife.net

Author **Casana Fink** is a liver recipient's daughter who has devoted herself to educating and promoting on organ and tissue donation for the past decade.

Since the age of 14, when she created her non-profit, **Give to Live - Donate Life**, she has been an ambassador for **Donate Life Florida** and traveled the state speaking to thousands of students, DMV employees, corporations, community members, and civic organizations. She has worked alongside legislators and transplant organizations to lobby and pass legislation to benefit the transplant community.

Every day her family is grateful to the donor that saved her father's life. She continues to devote herself to spreading awareness on this under-discussed, yet vital topic. As a recipient family member, it is her goal to continue to honor the selfless decision her father's donor made and to advocate for the over 100,000 people that are tirelessly waiting on the transplant list. It became evident to her that the demand for organs far outweighs the supply and that many individuals may never receive a call that they have an organ match.

She advocates fiercely to give these individuals hope, a second chance at life, and to no longer have to say goodbye to almost 20 of them each day.

Illustrator **Abbey Bryant**, is a New York City based children's artist. She creates bold, warm and textured digital work perfect for her adventurous story-telling and memorable characters. Most days she can be found around the city drawing New Yorkers or sketching at the park.

As a queer artist, Abbey specializes in inclusive projects that represent marginalized people and their stories.

See more of her books at **maddyabbs.com**.